Y0-CUL-814   SEP   2019

Journey to Joy's House
• Respecting Parents •

By T. M. Merk

Published by The Child's World®
1980 Lookout Drive • Mankato, MN 56003-1705
800-599-READ • www.childsworld.com

Photographs: Dan76/Shutterstock.com, cover, 1, 4, 7, 9, 12, 17, 19;
Monkey Business Images/Shutterstock.com, 11;
ismagination/Shutterstock.com, 14
Icons: © Aridha Prassetya/Dreamstime, 3, 7, 11, 12, 15, 22

Copyright ©2019 by The Child's World®
All rights reserved. No part of this book may be reproduced or utilized in any form or by any means without written permission from the publisher.

ISBN HARDCOVER: 9781503827455
ISBN PAPERBACK: 9781622434411
LCCN: 2017961936

Printed in the United States of America
PA02379

About the Author

T.M. Merk is an elementary educator with a master's degree in elementary education from Lesley University in Cambridge, Massachusetts. Drawing on years of classroom experience, she enjoys creating engaging educational material that inspires students' passion for learning. She lives in New Hampshire with her husband and her dog, Finn.

Table of Contents

Journey to Joy's House ---------- 5

Respectful Talk ---------- 20

S.T.E.A.M. Activity ---------- 21

Glossary ---------- 22

To Learn More ---------- 23

Index ---------- 24

Journey to Joy's House

It was almost time for school, but Joy wouldn't stop painting.

"Joy, please get dressed," her mother called. "We need to leave soon!"

"No! I'm busy right now!" Joy shouted back.

Leo the paintbrush wiggled in Joy's hand.

"Hi, Joy," he said. "You are not being respectful to your mother!"

Showing **respect** means that you show that you care about a person and his or her feelings. There are many ways to show respect. You can be a good listener, follow directions, and be polite. It was disrespectful when Joy said "no" to her mother.

"I'm not?" Joy asked. "But, Leo, I just want to keep painting."

"It's time to brush up on respect," Leo said. "Let's talk about respecting the people who care for you!"

"Your parents take care of you and keep you safe," Leo said. "They also teach you how to be **considerate** and kind. Your mother knows that going to school is best for you. You will learn new things and make friends."

Your parents help you make good choices about your health and safety. They teach you manners and **appropriate** behavior. They love you, and they want what is best for you.

Your parents often ask you to do things that you might not want to do, but they know that these things will help you to be a better *you*. Every day your parents help you to learn and grow.

"If my mother knows that school is good for me, I should care about it, right?" Joy asked.

"Right!" Leo said. "That's one way you can be respectful to your mother. You can also listen to her. Does she listen to you?"

Joy nodded. "She listens to me when I tell her about my paintings."

"Another part of being respectful to your mother is speaking kindly to her," Leo continued.

> Sometimes we don't notice that what we are saying is disrespectful or said with a poor attitude. Always take a moment to "think" before you speak. Is what you are saying **T**rue, **H**elpful, **I**nspiring, **N**ecessary, or **K**ind? If it is not any of those things, it is better left unsaid.

"I think you're right," said Joy. "I shouldn't shout at my mother or **argue** about what she asks me to do. I should be more helpful to her."

"Yes, that's it!" Leo said, smiling. "You'll see that when you show your parents the same respect that they show you, you'll all be happy!"

Respectful Talk

Do you need help talking in a respectful way to your parents? Use these sentence starters to help!

- May I please … ?
- Is now a good time for … ?
- Do you mind if I … ?
- After this, could we … ?
- I liked it when you said …
- May I please have a few more minutes to _____ before we _____ ?

S.T.E.A.M. Activity

Design a Tool That Makes Doing a Chore Easier

Directions: Using any materials that you choose, design a tool that makes a chore easier. The chore that you pick is up to you, but it should be something that is helpful to your parents.

Time Constraints: You may use a total of 30 minutes for your creation. You are allowed 10 minutes to plan and 20 minutes to build your tool. When you're done, test it to see if it works.

Discussion: Did you take time to think about what would be helpful to your parents? Did you practice "think" before you speak? Were your parents glad that you found a way to help? How did you feel when you were done? What worked really well? What could you do better next time?

Suggested Materials:
- Construction paper
- Pipe cleaners
- Tinfoil
- Popsicle sticks
- Toothpicks
- Tape
- Glue
- Safety scissors
- Markers/crayons

Glossary

appropriate: (uh-PROH-pree-it) When something is appropriate, it is right for a certain situation.

argue: (ARG-yoo) To argue is to disagree about something.

considerate: (kun-SIH-duh-rit) When you think about others and show kindness, you are considerate.

respect: (rih-SPEKT) To respect is to show that you care about a person, place, thing, or idea.

To Learn More

Books

Berenstain, Jan and Mike. *The Berenstain Bears Show Some Respect*. Grand Rapids, MI: Zonderkidz, 2011.

Cook, Julia. *The Worst Day of My Life Ever!: My Story about Listening and Following Instructions...(or Not!)*. Boys Town, NE: Boys Town Press, 2011.

Loewen, Nancy. *Treat Me Right!: Kids Talk About Respect.* Minneapolis, MN: Picture Window Books, 2002.

Web Sites

Visit our Web site for links about respecting your parents:
childsworld.com/links

Note to Parents, Teachers, and Librarians: We routinely verify our Web links to make sure they are safe and active sites. So encourage your readers to check them out!

Index

A
appropriate, 11

argue, 16

C
considerate, 10

L
listening, 13

P
parents, 10, 11, 12

R
respect, 7, 8, 18

T
T.H.I.N.K., 15